Bungalo Books

presenta

MORTIMER MOONER

STOPPED TAKING A BATH

Illustrated by John Bianchi

Written by Frank B. Edwards

On Monday, Mortimer Mooner stopped wearing a tie.

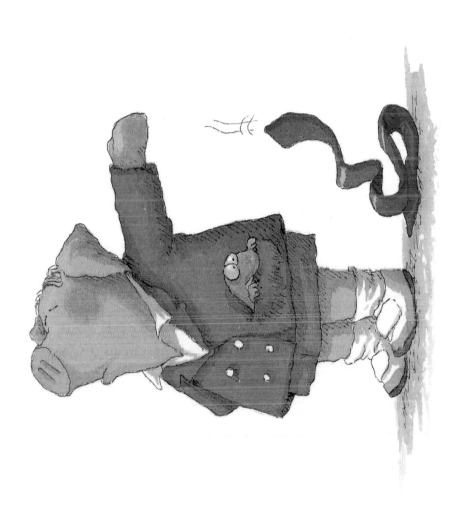

On Tuesday, a tieless Mortimer Mooner stopped cleaning his room.

On Wednesday, a messy Mortimer Mooner stopped washing his trotters.

On Thursday, a grimy
Mortimer Mooner stopped
combing his hair.

On Friday, a scruffy Mortimer Mooner stopped brushing his teeth.

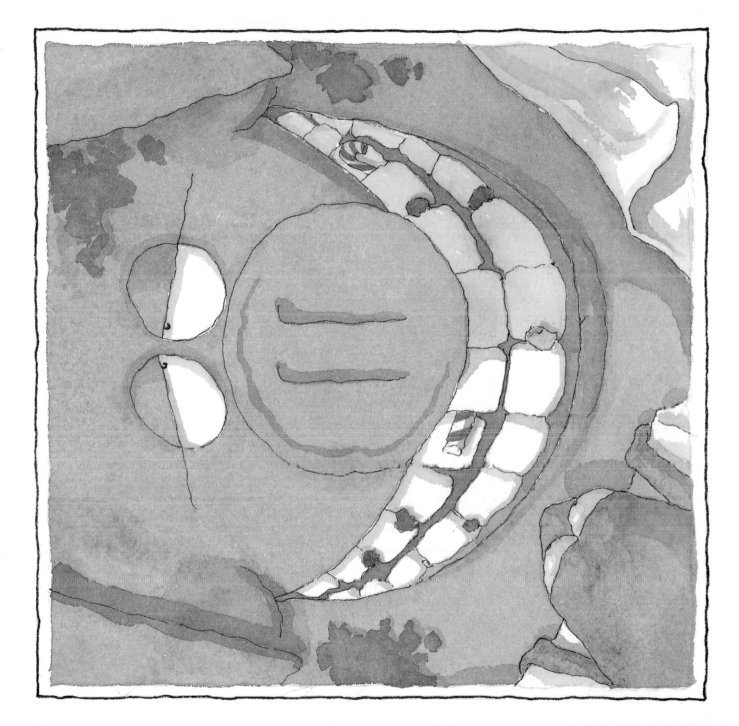

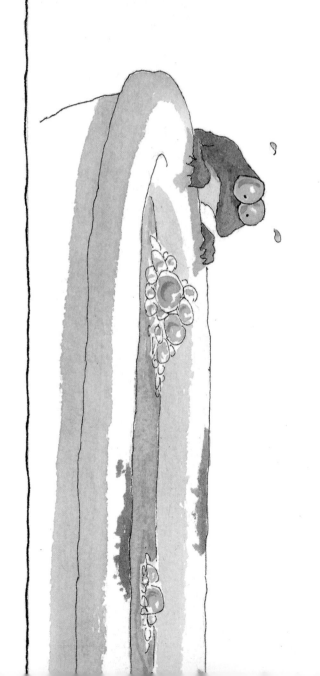

And on Saturday, a tieless, messy, grimy, scruffy, stinky Mortimer Mooner stopped taking a bath.

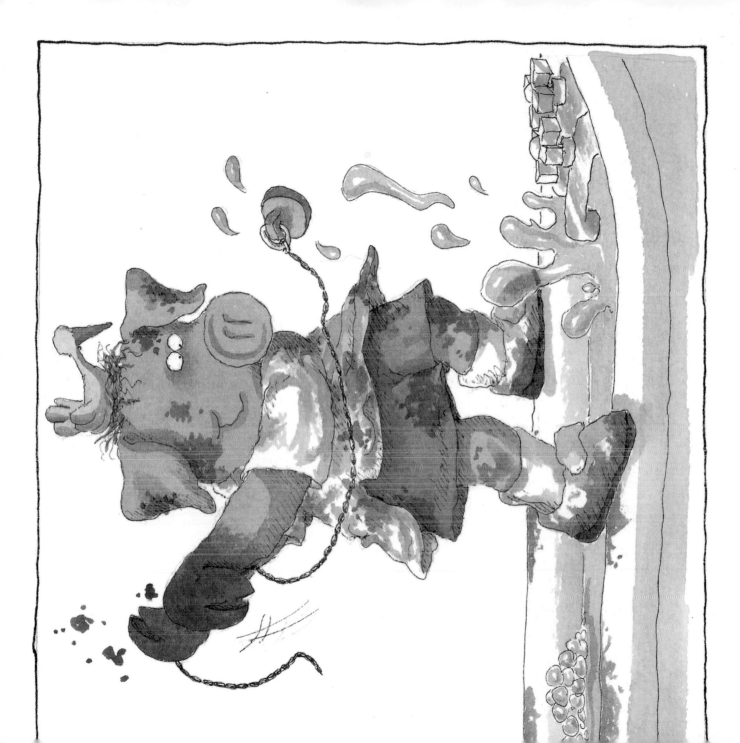

On Sunday, Mortimer Mooner received a visit from his grandmother and ran to give her a hug. But Grandmother Mooner held back.

She looked at his trotters and his hair and his teeth. She peered into his messy room. She even sniffed the air.

"My dear Mortimer," she said, "even though I do love you very much, I think that if I tried to hug you, I would surely faint."

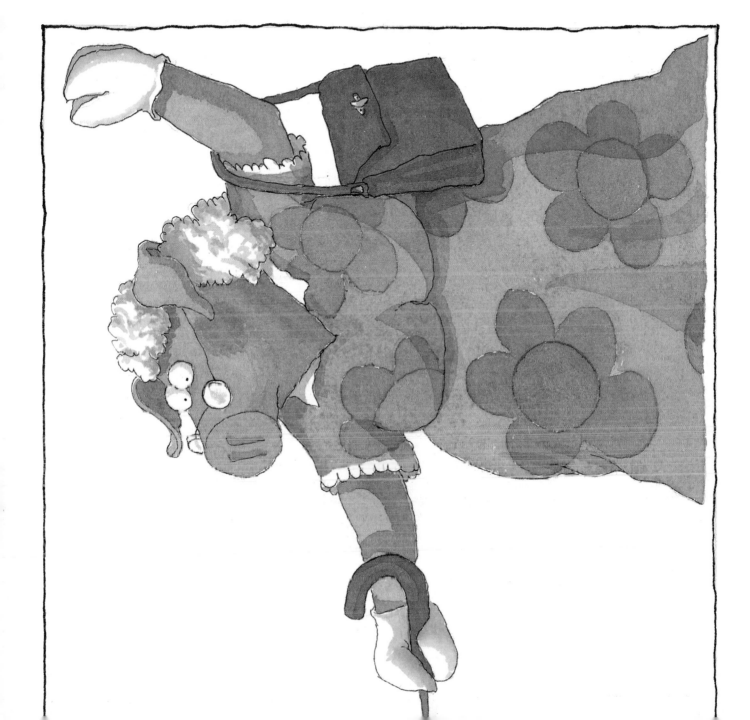

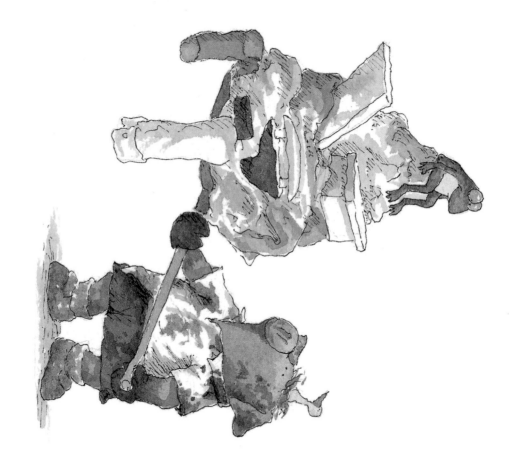

"Well," said Mortimer Mooner, "maybe I'll clean my room.

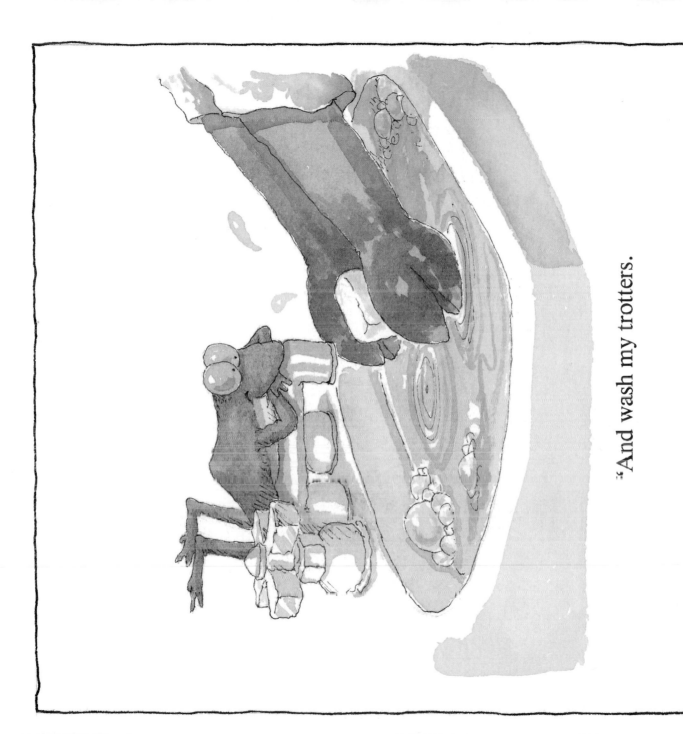

"And wash my trotters.

"And comb my hair.

"And brush my teeth.

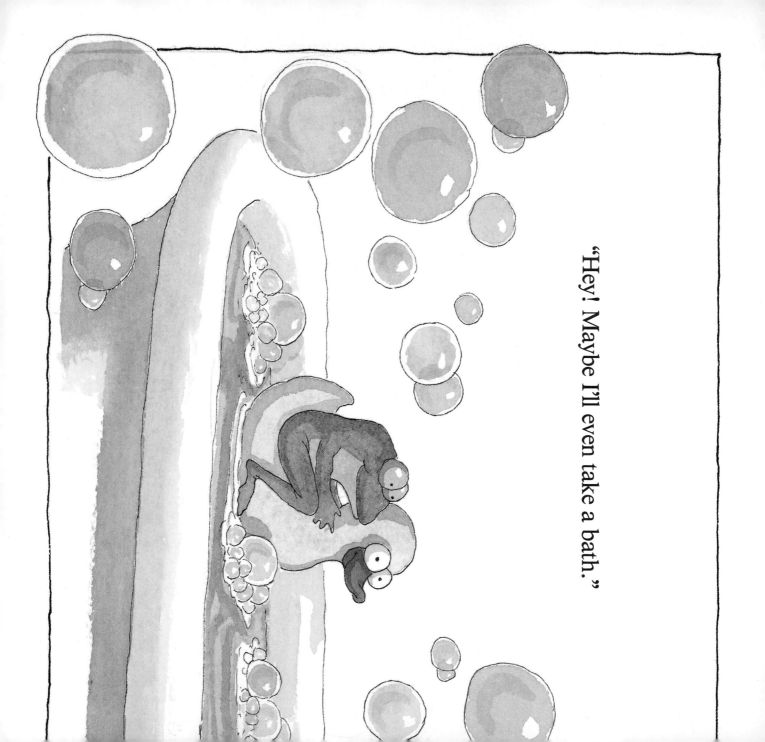

"Hey! Maybe I'll even take a bath."

And when he was done, his grand-mother gave him a hug and a kiss and made him some lunch.